'Scrooge meets the Lit...

LIST OF CHAR...

ROSIE	The poor little match girl.
EBENEZER SCROOGE	A covetous old sinner.
JACOB MARLEY	Scrooge's late partner.
GHOST OF CHRISTMAS PAST	
GHOST OF CHRISTMAS PRESENT	
GHOST OF CHRISTMAS YET TO COME	
BOB CRATCHIT	Scrooge's long suffering clerk.
MRS CRATCHIT	
TINY TIM	
BELINDA	
MARTHA	
PETER	
CHRISTABEL BONNE	Jolly charity worker.
HOLLY BONNE	Jolly charity worker.
TOM	Drunken reveller.
DICK	Drunken reveller.
HARRY	Drunken reveller.
BELLE	Scrooge's one and only sweetheart.
HUSBAND	Belle's husband
MR FEZZIWIG	A kind-hearted, jovial old merchant.
MRS FEZZIWIG	A worthy partner of Mr Fezziwig.
DICK WILKINS	A fellow apprentice of Scrooge's.
OLD JOE	A receiver of stolen goods.
MRS DILBER	A laundress.
MR SMITH	An undertaker's man.
MRS WIDDLE	A charwoman.
FRED	Scrooge's nephew.
BETTY	Fred's wife.
FAN	Scrooge's sister.
JIM	Debtor.
CAROLINE	Debtor.
BUSINESSMAN # 1	
BUSINESSMAN # 2	
FATHER	
MOTHER	
DAUGHTER	
BLIND MAN	
SAILOR	
CAPTAIN	
CHOIR / PHANTOMS	

Act I

Scene 1

A snow bedecked small town centre with an ornate Christmas Tree.

A Group of CAROL SINGERS, well wrapped in hats, gloves and scarves sing merrily away. A large town house with windows overlooks the square. They sing 'In the Bleak Mid-Winter.'

CAROL SINGERS   In the bleak mid-winter, frosty wind made moan. Earth stood hard as iron, water like a stone. Snow had fallen, snow on snow, snow on snow. In the bleak mid- winter, long ago…

A small little girl, dressed in rags, and obviously cold, ROSIE, sits in the office doorway of 'Scrooge and Marley'. She tries, unsuccessfully, to sell matches to passers-by, some of whom are carrying lots of shopping, food and presents.

ROSIE   Matches! Matches! Matches for sale!

A well to do FATHER and MOTHER, with a little GIRL wander by. Rosie smiles at the Girl. The Girl turns her nose up at ROSIE, and walks on.

Rosie *rubs her hands to keep warm.*

The Carol Singers finish their song and start to move off to another part of town.

A bedraggled young clerk opens the door to the office: BOB CRATCHIT.

He looks at Rosie *and delves deep into his pockets. He retrieves a solitary coin and hand sit to her. She hands him a box of matches with a smile.*

ROSIE   Merry Christmas, Mr Cratchit!

BOB   Merry Christmas, Rosie.

He looks worriedly around and scuttles off into the dark.

An old BLIND MAN passes by rattling a tin. He is ignored by the throng.

Rosie places her one and only coin in his hand. He bows.

ROSIE   Happy Christmas, Sir!

BLIND MAN   Thank you, Miss.

Rosie *smiles graciously and recoils embarrassed to her step.*

A grumpy old man starts walking towards Rosie, SCROOGE. *He bustles through the midst of the Carol Singers and starts mumbling to himself. He continually waves his walking stick to keep humanity at bay.*

SCROOGE   Bah Humbug!

ROSIE   Matches. *Beat*. Matches for sale!

Scrooge scowls at Rosie as he clears her with his foot from his office doorstep. She looks at him pleadingly.

ROSIE   Happy Christmas Mr Scrooge! Matches for your fire?

SCROOGE   Get away with you, beggar!

He scowls once more and slams the door as he enters.

Rosie *places her hands under her armpits and looks forlornly at the Christmas Tree.*

Rosie *starts to sob.*

A Spectre appears on the stage, MARLEY, bedecked in chains, and shakes his head in disappointment.

He pats her on the head, but she is unaware of his gesture.

She looks around and takes a match guiltily from her wares, lights it, and cups her hands around the fleeting warmth.

Scene 2

Scrooge's office. Spartan furniture, two desks, one small with a large ledger, Bob Cratchit's; and his own, a large desk, loaded with papers. A rocking chair sits under a grandfather clock, to one side.

Scrooge lights a candle with a match, sits at a table and starts wading through his ledgers with meticulous detail. A portrait of Marley sits behind his desk – ever watchful. The eyes of the portrait are hollow and perhaps move as they watch Scrooge at work.

Bob Cratchit stands and waves his arms in an attempt to get warm.

SCROOGE   Sit down Scratchit and get on with your work. This is an office not a gymnasium.

CRATCHIT   May I light the fire Mr Scrooge?

SCROOGE   You'll burn in hell for your laziness young man. You'll be warm then all right. Ha! Get on with your work. I want those debtor's letters out by tonight.

Bob Cratchit starts scribbling away furiously in his ledger.

CRATCHIT   It's Christmas Eve, sir– surely it would be better if we waited until the new year?

SCROOGE   Hah Humbug! Christmas! I'll not have them frittering away my money on festivities and presents. It's a waste of time I tell you.

Cratchit continues labouring at the ledger. Scrooge scowls and resumes his counting. The door opens and FRED, Scrooge's nephew enters with an air of joviality.

FRED	A merry Christmas, Uncle! God save you!

Fred tries to shake hands with his uncle but is rebuffed.

SCROOGE	Bah! Humbug!
FRED	Come now uncle – Christmas a humbug, you can't mean it surely?
SCROOGE	I do. What have you got to be so happy about? You're poor enough…
FRED	Then why are you miserable? You're rich enough…
CRATCHIT	Touché!

Scrooge silences Cratchit with a glare and he resumes his writing.

FRED	A merry Christmas to you, Mr Cratchit! I trust you are celebrating the day tomorrow. You do have the day free I'm sure?
CRATCHIT	Merry Christmas! *Pause*. I have not dared ask yet, Master Fred.
FRED	The office will be closed anyway as my uncle will be dining chez moi!
SCROOGE	Hah! I most certainly will not. There is too much to be done here. I will not fritter away my time as you do.
FRED	Don't be so angry uncle. Dine with us tomorrow?

SCROOGE	Still married then?
FRED	Of course.
SCROOGE	Why? *Beat.* Why get married?
FRED	Love!
SCROOGE	Bah! Love! Hah! Good day to you nephew.
FRED	I want nothing from you but your good company. Do come. Why cannot we be friends?
SCROOGE	Good day, sir!
FRED	We have no quarrel, so I give you my best wishes again. *Beat.* Merry Christmas, uncle!
SCROOGE	Good day!

Fred disappears around the door way. He then pops his head around cheekily the corner again.

FRED	And a happy new year!
SCROOGE	Good day!

Miss CHRISTABEL and Miss HOLLY Bonne, two rosy cheeked matrons, enter before the door shuts.

HOLLY	You are a popular man! Season's greetings!
CHRISTABEL	Do we have the pleasure of addressing Mr Marley, or Mr Scrooge?

SCROOGE	There is no pleasure here. Mr Marley has been dead these seven years now. (*He drifts off for a moment*). He died seven years ago, this very night…

Scrooge indicates the portrait above his desk.

CHRISTABEL	Mr Scrooge then, season's greetings!
SCROOGE	Bah! Leave me in peace.
HOLLY	It is peace that we bring you. Holly Bonne.
CHRISTABEL	Christabel Bonne.

The two sisters curtsy. Bob Cratchit bows. Scrooge places his head in his hand.

HOLLY	At this time of the year it is important that we think of those less fortunate than ourselves: the poor.
CHRISTABEL	The poor poor.
HOLLY	Many thousands are in need of common comforts. We should make provision for them lest they perish in the cold.
CHRISTABEL	So cold.
SCROOGE	Are there no shelters?
CHRISTABEL	Plenty.
SCROOGE	Workhouses too?
HOLLY	Many.
SCROOGE	Prisons?

CHRISTBEL	Too many!
SCROOGE	I am glad to hear it.
CHRISTABEL	We are trying to raise funds for the unfortunates. We mean to buy them food, drink and a little warmth. We choose now, above all times as this is when Want is keenly felt and Abundance rejoices. What shall we put you down for?
SCROOGE	Nothing!
HOLLY	You wish to remain anonymous?
CHRISTABEL	Sweet man!
SCROOGE	I wish to be left alone. I do not make merry at Christmas myself and I have neither the means nor desire to make idle people merry. I contribute to the establishments I mentioned – they cost enough: and those that are badly off should go there.
CHRISTABEL	Many can't go there; and many would rather die.
SCROOGE	If they would rather die, then they had better do so and decrease the surplus population. I do not care about them.
HOLLY	But now you are aware of their plight, surely…
SCROOGE	It's not my business. My business occupies my time, and on that note, you should leave. Good day, ladies.
HOLLY	But think of the cold, you have a cold heart Mr Scrooge.

CHRISTABEL   Cold dear heart!

Christabel makes a move to hug Scrooge and he sidesteps her advances. Cratchit stifles a chuckle. Holly produces a sprig of mistletoe and makes a move to other side of the desk intent on a kiss.

SCROOGE   Get away from me you harlots!

The two sisters step back in shock and Scrooge stands on his desk and shoos them away. They head for the door where Bob Cratchit sees them out with a gentle bow. Scrooge sits back at his desk and tries to resume his work.

SCROOGE   You see Scratchit, madness; this is the season of utter folly. It will be over soon…

CRATCHIT   While we are discussing the season of goodwill I was wondering…

SCROOGE   Oh yes?

There is the sound of drunken carol singers from outside, 'Jingle Bells' being sung very badly, followed by the appearance of three revellers, TOM, DICK, and HARRY. They are drunk as lords and intent on fun with Scrooge.

TOM, DICK and HARRY   Jingle all the way, oh what fun is to have old Scroogey Boy on our Sleigh!

DICK   Season's greeting's, Bobby!

Bob Cratchit smiles nervously. The three men turn their attentions to Scrooge.

HARRY   Evening your happiness!

TOM   Penny for the Guy?

DICK   And what would you like for Christmas young man?

Scrooge fixes them with an icy glaze, Harry offers him some grog. He shakes his head and then looks at his late partner's portrait.

SCROOGE   All I wish is to be left alone.

Bob Cratchit ushers the revellers to the door. The singing continues off down the street.

SCROOGE   What a nightmare, the world has gone bonkers: beggars, brazen women, and binge drinkers. *Pause.* Have you finished those reminders?

CRATCHIT   Almost Mr Scrooge. About tomorrow?

SCROOGE   You'll want all tomorrow off, I suppose?

CRATCHIT   If that's convenient, sir?

SCROOGE   It is neither convenient nor fair. I suppose you expect to be paid for it too? *Beat.* Yet you don't think me ill-used when you pick my pocket of a day's ages every twenty fifth of December!

CRATCHIT   Me and mine would be most grateful Mr Scrooge, sir.

SCROOGE   Deliver those letters on you way home and be here all the earlier the next morning. I shall be working here to make up for lost time.

Bob Cratchit folds his last envelope and grabs his hat and scarf.

CRATCHIT   Merry Christmas, Mr Scrooge!

As he exits we can still hear Rosie the little match girl, selling her wares.

SCROOGE   Shut the door firmly on your way out.

He peers out of the window at her and grows angry. He opens the door and shouts ferociously at her.

SCROOGE   Away with you girl. Some of us still have work to do.

Scrooge slams the door and yet there is still the cry of Rosie calling out 'Matches?' from his doorstep.

SCROOGE   Youngsters today – no respect!

He settles by his desk and resumes his work. Apart from the faint cry of 'Matches', all is quiet.

Marley's spectre enters through the door.

Marley pinches out the candle without Scrooge noticing him. Scrooge looks up from his ledger and mutters a sigh. The door flaps in the wind.

SCROOGE   Scratchit? Is that you? You sciving scumbag. I won't give you an advance to waste on your family. I won't, do you hear?

Scrooge slams the door shut and heads towards his desk; in the gloom he still does not notice that the portrait seems to have come alive. Marley is standing directly in front of it and indeed it has.

Scrooge strikes another match, lights the candle and carries on his accounting. Marley is staring at him with disdain from behind his chair.

Marley blows the candle out and sweeps the coins and ledgers across the floor.

Marley rattles his chains. Scrooge looks around.

Scrooge is torn what to do. He reaches for his walking stick, waving it blindly.

SCROOGE   Thieves! Madmen! Help me somebody!

Marley lights the candle and glares at his former partner.

MARLEY   I am here to help you Ebeneezer Scrooge!

Scrooge shudders, twists and turns. The sound of grim laments and moans emanate from all bouts. He frantically bolts the door and stands with his back to it. The moans rise to a crescendo then cease.

MARLEY   You have eyes but you do not see.

SCROOGE   I know that voice. You are an impostor! What trick is this?

Scrooge swipes at Marley who dodges him deftly. Scrooge watches his former partner warily.

SCROOGE   What do you want with me?

MARLEY   Much!

SCROOGE   Who are you?

MARLEY   Ask me who I *was*?

SCROOGE   Who were you then?

MARLEY   In life I was your partner, Jacob Marley.

SCROOGE   Can you, *Beat,* can you sit down?

MARLEY   I can.

SCROOGE   Do it then.

Marley sits in the rocking chair, quite at home.

MARLEY   You don't believe in me.

SCROOGE   I do not.

MARLEY	What more evidence do you need that that of your own senses?
SCROOGE	Because they can be affected. A fever, a slight disorder of the stomach? Yes that could be it: an underdone potato, a crumb of cheese, an undigested piece of beef…*Beat. (Starts to cackle)* There's more of gravy than of grave about you, whatever you are!

Marley sat stock still and watched Scrooge cease his giggling. He starts to unravel a bandage about his head and an eyeball drops to the floor. Marley starts to laugh uproariously at Scrooge's disgust and terror. The phantoms shriek and clamour.

Marley stands up and Scrooge falls to his knees with his hands clasped penitently.

SCROOGE	Mercy! Oh dreadful apparition. Why do you trouble me?
MARLEY	Do you believe in me in not?
SCROOGE	I do, I must. But why do spirits walk the earth, and why visit me?
MARLEY	It is required of every man that the spirit within him should walk abroad among his fellow-men, and travel far and wide; and, if that spirit goes forth not in life, then it is condemned to after death. It must witness what it can no longer share, but might have shared on earth, and turned to happiness.

Marley raises his arms in anguish to heaven, they are weighed in chains. He moans and lets out a cry.

MARLEY	Woe is me! Despair, despair…
SCROOGE	You are fettered, why?

MARLEY	I wear the chain I forged in life. Link by link, yard by yard and inch by miserable inch. I girded it of my own free will and of my own free will I wore it. Do you not feel the weight of you very own? It grows, and grows still yet Ebenezer Scrooge. It was full and heavy as this seven Christmas Eves ago. You have laboured on it since. It is a ponderous chain!
SCROOGE	Jacob. Jacob Marley, my old friend. Speak comfort to me.
MARLEY	I have none to give, nor can I rest. I cannot linger anywhere. My very own spirit never walked beyond our counting house – mark me – in life my spirit never roved beyond the narrow limits of profit. Now only endless journeys lie before me.
SCROOGE	You must travel very slowly Jacob.
MARLEY	Slowly?
SCROOGE	Seven years dead and still travelling?
MARLEY	The whole time, no rest, no peace. Incessant torture and remorse.
SCROOGE	You must have been to a good many places on your journeys…
MARLEY	Oh! You labour on your very own chains. Captive of the counting house, set thyself free! Not to know that no space of regret can make amends for one life's opportunity misused! Yet such was I! Oh such was I!
SCROOGE	You, no! No man was more solid and good in business.

MARLEY	Business! Mankind was my business. The common welfare was my business: charity, mercy, forbearance. These were all my business. *Pause.* It is now, at this time of year that I suffer most.
SCROOGE	It's only one day…
MARLEY	Listen to me! My time is nearly gone. Why did I walk through the crowds of fellow beings with my eyes turned away? The blessed star that led the Wise Men to the poor abode. Were there no poor homes to which its light might have guided me?
SCROOGE	But Jacob…
MARLEY	Hear me!
SCROOGE	I will, but don't be too hard on me, I beg of you.
MARLEY	I have sat invisible by your side many, many a day. How you may see me now is a mystery. I am here tonight to warn you that there is still time, there is a chance that you might escape my fate…
SCROOGE	You were always a good friend to me. Thank you!
MARLEY	You will be haunted by Three Spirits.
SCROOGE	Is that it? What about the chance and hope you spoke of?
MARLEY	It is.
SCROOGE	I think I'd rather not, if that's all the same…

MARLEY	Without their visits you cannot hope to shun the path I tread. Expect the first tomorrow, when the bell tolls one.
SCROOGE	Let's not drag this out. Couldn't they come at the same time and get it out the way? It's been a long day.
MARLEY	Expect the second on the next night at the same hour. The third, upon the next night when the last stroke of twelve has ceased to vibrate. *Pause.* Look to see me no more; and see that, for your own sake, Ebenezer Scrooge, remember what has passed between us.

Marley re-bandages his head and stoops to pick up his eyeball. He winks at Scrooge and his partner looks on, at a loss for words. Marley starts to walk backwards towards the door. Scrooge starts to follow, mesmerised. Marley holds up a hand indicating for Scrooge to stop. He does.

The door and windows start to rattle and the phantoms appear, wailing and crying. They fill the room and dance around Scrooge. He covers his ears and eyes, screaming. Marley is obscured and is gone by the time the gruesome phantoms leave Scrooge to his fate. Scrooge stands still, looks about him and races to the door. It is still bolted. There is a knock at the door. He opens it slowly, his cane at the ready. Rosie is standing there, shivering.

ROSIE	Is everything all right Mr Scrooge?
SCROOGE	Of course. *Pause.* Why do you ask?
ROSIE	Only I heard screaming.
SCROOGE	Ummm! Must be cats.

He looks at this sorry creature and there is almost a flicker of pity.

ROSIE	Good night then, Mr Scrooge.
SCROOGE	Don't you have a home to go to? *Pause.* Are you going to sleep in my doorway?
ROSIE	I'll move if you want sir.
SCROOGE	No. No, that's fine. Goodnight.
ROSIE	Merry Christmas!

Scrooge peers behind her and then shuts the door. He bolts it and double checks it. He places on a nightcap and sits in the rocking chair under his old coat, his cane by his side. Scrooge peers up above the coat and scans the room.

SCROOGE	Humbug!

Scrooge pulls the cap over his eyes and tries for sleep.

Act II

Scene 1

Scrooge is in a deep slumber. The clock dials starts to spin and stops at twelve.

He awakes and peers about him, then intently at the clock.

SCROOGE   Midnight! *Beat.* Why it isn't possible. Perhaps it is noon?

He scrambles out of the chair, shivers, and makes for the window. It is night. He checks the door for peace of mind and returns to his rocking chair.

SCROOGE   Was it a dream or not? No. Executive stress…

He makes himself cosy in the rocking chair and as he closes his eyes the clock starts whirring. He stares at it…It spins and chimes a quarter past.

SCROOGE   A quarter past

It whirrs to half past and tolls…

SCROOGE   Half past

It whirrs to quarter to and chimes…

SCROOGE   A quarter to it

It whirrs to one o'clock…

SCROOGE   The hour itself and nothing! Hah!

As the bell strikes one the room lights up and a hand appears by his side. Scrooge recoils from it, then the apparition makes itself clear: A child, yet with an old face, white hair and holding a sprig of holly in its hand.

SCROOGE	Are you the spirit child? The spirit whose coming was foretold to me?
PAST	I am.
SCROOGE	Who, or rather, what are you?
PAST	I am the Ghost of Christmas Past.
SCROOGE	Long past?
PAST	No. *Beat.* Your past.
SCROOGE	No thank you. It does not do to look backwards – onward, ever onward is my mantra.
PAST	Is that so?
SCROOGE	Why are you here spirit?
PAST	Your welfare.
SCROOGE	Well, the best thing for me would be a good night's sleep so goodnight child. You may go!

Scrooge seeks the sanctuary of his coat. The spirit grows impatient, and pulls it to the floor.

PAST	Your salvation then. Take heed!

The spirit takes him by the arm.

PAST	Rise and walk with me!

The spirit leads Scrooge to the sidelines and raises his arms enveloping all in darkness.

Scene 2

A schoolroom. Boys race out of the room merrily and bid each other a 'Happy Holiday!'

SCROOGE	Valentine and his brother Orson. There they go!
PAST	These are but shadows of the things that have been. They have no consciousness of us.
SCROOGE	I know this place. My schoolroom!
PAST	The school is not fully deserted.

A solitary boy Scrooge is left at his desk, a case by his side. He watches his friends depart into the arms of their families.

PAST	Your lip is trembling, and what is that upon your cheek?

Scrooge wipes his cheek and clears his throat.

SCROOGE	Dust in my eye.
PAST	Poor boy!
SCROOGE	I wish…
PAST	Yes?
SCROOGE	There was a child at my door last night, a little match girl. I should have bought some: that's all.

The spirit smiles thoughtfully and waves its arm.

PAST	Let us see another Christmas.

The room grows dark.

Scene 3

Little Scrooge is still at his desk. He gets up and starts pacing fretfully.

A little girl, Fran, enters the room and Scrooge's eyes light up.

FRAN	I have come to bring you home, dear brother.
BOY SCROOGE	Home little Fran?
FRAN	Home for good, home for ever and ever. Father is so much kinder than he used to be. I asked him if you could come home this year and he agreed.
BOY SCROOGE	You are sure?
FRAN	You are never to come back here. We're to be together all Christmas long.
BOY SCROOGE	You are quite the little woman, Fran.

They embrace. He grabs his little case and they head merrily out of the schoolroom, she drags him by the hand in her eagerness.

PAST	Always a delicate creature, whom a breath might have withered. But she had a large heart!
SCROOGE	So she had spirit. You're right.
PAST children?	She died a young woman and had, as I think,
SCROOGE	One child.

PAST	True, your nephew.
SCROOGE	Yes.

The room grows dark as the spirit waves its arm.

Scene 4

A decorated and glowing office – Fezziwig's. Young Scrooge and his fellow apprentice, Dick Wilkins, hard at work. Jovial Mr Fezziwig enters with a bottle and glasses.

FEZZIWIG	Yo Ho, my boys. No more work tonight, it's Christmas Eve!
PAST	Know this place?
SCROOGE	Know it! Was I not apprenticed here?
PAST	You were.
SCROOGE	Why it's old Dick Wilkins and old Fezziwig. Bless his heart, it's old Fezziwig, alive again! A kinder boss no man could want!
PAST	You were a good apprentice?

Scrooge reaches out to touch his jolly boss.

PAST	Shadows of what was…

Scrooge ruefully withdraws his hand.

FEZZIWIG	Dick, Ebenezer, take a glass for a toast.

Mrs Fezziwig enters brandishing a large knife and an enormous cake.

MRS FEZZIWIG	I hope you are hungry my lads!

Old Fezziwig pours them all a drink and they toast.

ALL			Merry Christmas!

Mrs Fezziwig then takes out a sprig of mistletoe and chases one and all about the office. She eventually catches old Fezziwig and gives him a soppy kiss. Dick Wilkins and Ebenezer Scrooge applaud.

A fiddler enters and the Fezziwigs dance while the apprentices clap.

PAST			So cheerful over such a small matter!

SCROOGE		Small!

PAST			Why, he has spent but a few pounds of your mortal money – three or four at most. Is that so much that he deserves such praise?

SCROOGE		It isn't that spirit. It is that he has the power to render us happy or unhappy; to make our service light or burdensome; a pleasure or a toil. The happiness he gives is quite as great as if it cost a fortune.

The spirit watches him.

PAST			What is the matter?

SCROOGE		Nothing!

PAST			Something, I think?

SCROOGE		No, well, I would like to be able to say a word to my clerk just now. That's all.

PAST			My time grows short. Quick!

The spirit waves his arms and all is dark.

Scene 5

A sweet girl, Belle, is revealed sitting deep in thought. The spirit casts a glance in Scrooge's direction and notices his agitation.

SCROOGE   You go to far!

PAST   Take heed! Time is short.

Belle starts to sob and the young Scrooge is not sure what to do.

BELLE   Another idol has displaced me.

YOUNG SCROOGE Which idol?

BELLE   A golden one.

YOUNG SCROOGE It is the dealings of the world. There is nothing so hard as poverty, yet you cast condemnation in the pursuit of wealth.

BELLE   You fear the world too much. All your other hopes have merged into the one of being beyond its sordid reproach. I have seen your nobler aspirations fall off, one by one, until the master passion – Gain, obsesses you. Is this not true?

YOUNG SCROOGE What of it? I have grown wiser to the world. I am not changed towards you.

Belle slowly shakes her head.

YOUNG SCROOGE Am I?

BELLE   Our contract is an old one. It was made when we were both poor, and content to be so, until, with time, we could improve our lot by patient industry. When it was made you were another man.

YOUNG SCROOGE   Oh Belle, I was a boy!

BELLE   That which was promised when we were of one heart, I will not bind you to, now that we are two. How often have I thought of this and will not say. It is enough that I have thought of it, and can release you.

YOUNG SCROOGE   Have I ever sought release?

BELLE   In words, no, never.

YOUNG SCROOGE   How then?

BELLE   In a changed nature, an altered spirit, another hope. Tell me, would you seek me out and try and win me now? *Beat.* Ahhh! No!

YOUNG SCROOGE   You think not.

BELLE   I would gladly think otherwise if I could. Heaven know! *Pause.* If you were fee today, tomorrow, yesterday, can even I believe that you would choose a dowerless girl – you who, in your very confidence with her, weigh everything by gain.

Belle eyes young Scrooge wearily. He shuffles and plays with his hands.

BELLE   I release you Ebenezer Scrooge. With a full heart, for the love of him you once were.

YOUNG SCROOGE   But…

BELLE	You may have pain for a while, a brief while; then you will dismiss the memory of it gladly, as an unprofitable dream, from which you are glad you awoke. *Pause.* May you be happy in the life you have chosen!

Belle walks off without a backward glance, her eyes wet with tears. Young Scrooge stands still and takes a breath, fighting his better nature.

Scrooge makes after her, the spirit takes his arm.

PAST	Shadows.
SCROOGE	But…
PAST	Hold! She is but a shadow of the past…

Scrooge watches her go and places a hand to his heart.

SCROOGE	Spirit – show me no more. Take me home. Why do you delight is torturing me so?
PAST	One shadow more!
SCROOGE	No more! I don't wish to see it! Show me no more!

The spirit waves his arms and all is dark.

Scene 6

Belle is in the rocking chair with a young baby. Her husband enters and takes off his hat and scarf.

Scrooge scowls at the spirit.

26

HUSBAND	Belle. *Beat.* I saw an old friend of yours this afternoon.
BELLE	Who was it?
HUSBAND	Guess.

The husband adopts a miserly hunch and glares at her. Belle giggles.

BELLE	I have no idea! Who was it?
HUSBAND	Mr Scrooge!

Scrooge looks at the floor. The spirit places a finger under his chin, forcing him to endure.

HUSBAND	I passed his office window and it was not shut, oh no, not even tonight. His partner lies at death's door and yet he sat alone at work. Quite alone in the world, I do believe.

The husband joins his wife and child; they hug. Scrooge's pain is palpable.

SCROOGE	Spirit. Remove me from this place!
PAST	I told you these were shadows of the things that have been. They are what they are, do not blame me!
SCROOGE	Remove me! I cannot bear it!

The spirit and Scrooge look at each other.

Pause.

SCROOGE	Leave me! Take me back. Haunt me no longer!

The spirit waves its arms and darkness prevails.

Scene 7

Scrooge is alone in his rocking chair, his coat about him, in a fitful sleep.

There is a set of spooky noises – scratching at the window pane, knocking on the walls – Scrooge grows ever more fitful and cries out.

He looks about him and then sticks his head under the pillow.

Act III

Scene 1

Scrooge snuffles and snores beneath his old coat. The clock hands start to spin. Scrooge awakes and stares at it.

It stops at midnight and progresses through the quarters to the allotted hour.

The clock tolls one o'clock and yet no spirit has appeared. He is determined not be taken unawares, however, and starts to prowl his offices, stick in hand, mumbling to himself.

A light starts to throb like a heart beat from the office door.

Scrooge sighs and approaches warily, drawing back the lock.

PRESENT (O/S) Ebenezer Scrooge?

Scrooge shivers and tenses. He opens the door and is taken by the hand, dragged through the threshold.

Scene 2

The Ghost of Christmas present is a jolly spirit with a green velvet suit, trimmed in white fur, a protruding belly, and a head bedecked in holly. He shakes Scrooge's hand with gusto. Scrooge's eyes remain downcast.

PRESENT	Come in! Come in! And know me better man!
SCROOGE	Ebenezer Scrooge. How do you…
PRESENT	(*Guffawing*) I know who you are!
SCROOGE	I am the ghost of Christmas Present. Look upon me.

Scrooge looks reverently at the second of the spirits.

PRESENT   You have never seen the like of me before!

SCROOGE   Never!

PRESENT   Some two thousand or more of my brothers have passed this way before me. Have ye not met them?

SCROOGE   I don't think so. That's a large family to provide for! How do you make do?

The spirit cackles and slaps him on the back so hard that Scrooge stumbles.

SCROOGE   Oh spirit. Please let this lesson be short! Lead me where you will but if you have aught to teach me. Let me profit by it…

PRESENT   Profit eh? *Beat.* Hah! Touch my robe.

Scrooge complies and throws sparkling dust in the air. There is the sound of a fearsome wind that brings darkness and a flurry of snow.

Scene 3

The spirit throws another handful of 'sparkle'. The world is alight with revellers, the spirit taking an obvious glee in their revelry. Tom, Dick and Harry share a bottle of cider as they sing by the tree. A poor couple hurry home gleefully with a cake.

The little match girl, Rosie, sits in Scrooge's doorway, shivering, hungry, and ignored. She strikes a match and warms herself, lost in the moment of reverie.

SCROOGE   Is there a particular flavour to your sprinkle?

PRESENT   There is. *Beat.* My own!

SCROOGE	Would it apply to any dinner given on this day?
PRESENT	To any kindly given. *Beat.* To a poor one the most.
SCROOGE	Why a poor one the most?
PRESENT	Because it needs it the most.

The spirit leans towards the little match girl and sprinkles his dust over her. A bread roll drops into her hand. She looks up, unaware from whence it came. She looks at it and decides to save it for later. She searches for her benefactor but speaks into 'thin air'.

ROSIE	Thank you. *Beat.* I make it last, I promise.
SCROOGE	Spirit, I wonder, that you, of all the beings about us in the world, should desire these people's opportunities of innocent enjoyment.
PRESENT	I?
SCROOGE	You seek to close places of endeavour every seventh day, thereby preventing honest income…
PRESENT	I seek?
SCROOGE	Forgive me if I am wrong, but it has been done in your name, at least in the name of your family…
PRESENT	There are some upon this earth of yours, who *claim* to know us, the spirits and who do their wicked deeds: ill-will, hatred, envy, bigotry, and selfishness in our name, who are strange to us, and all our kith and kin...

Scrooge shivers and shakes with fear.

PRESENT	Remember that, and charge their actions on them, not us.
SCROOGE	I will.
PRESENT	Behold!

The spirit sprinkles his dust and the scene is plunged into darkness.

SCROOGE (O/S)	Aitchooo!
PRESENT (O/S)	Bless you!

Scene 4

Bob Cratchit's dwelling: Mrs Cratchit in a poor robe done up as best she can with ribbons. Belinda Cratchit, again in shreds and bows, lays the dinner table, coveting a large red candle that is to be the centre piece of their festivities.

Peter Cratchit stirs the pot. Martha bursts in from outside, holding a goose, stripping off her bonnet and scarf as she grips her siblings in an embrace. She hands the goose to her mother.

MARTHA	We finished early! *Beat.* This was the last one left!
MRS CRATCHIT	Hide! You father would never guess at such a gift.
PETER	Where is father and Tiny Tim?
MRS CRATCHIT	He'll be free at the last minute, we know that...
BELINDA	Here comes father! *Beat.* Quick Martha hide!

Martha steals herself behind a curtain and holds her breath. Bob Cratchit enters with Tiny Tim at his side, hobbling stoically on a crutch.

MRS CRATCHIT	You two! Been partying again?
TINY TIM	Yes, Mother! We saw a tree and the spirit of Christmas!
BOB	It was magnificent!
MRS CARTCHIT	The spirit?
TINY TIM	The tree!
BOB	The spirit was there too – in spirit anyway!
TINY TIM	Where's Martha?
MRS CRATCHIT	Shops nowadays. You know how it is…
BOB	But it's Christmas Day!
PETER	Exactly! A feast for fools!
BOB	Then we are a ship of fools! We will wait for Martha.
PETER	Set sail ma!
TINY TIM	No!
MRS CRATCHIT	Bon Appetit!

The family sits down and bowed their heads and waited for Bob Cratchit to say the blessing. He cannot.

BOB	We must wait for Martha.
TINY TIM	Let's find her.

BELINDA	*(Giggling)* She isn't far!

Bob Cratchit guesses the game and starts to hunt for his daughter. There are shouts of 'warm' and 'cold' as he paces about the room. Scrooge grows excited and calls out to.

SCROOGE	Behind the curtain!
PRESENT	You have not earned your place here at their table, they cannot hear you. They are but shadows…
SCROOGE	I pay him, even on his days off…

The spirit glares at him and Scrooge cannot meet his gaze.

SCROOGE	How could I know about his family?
PRESENT	You could inquire…
SCROOGE	But we are so busy with business…
PRESENT	Mankind is our business!
SCROOGE	Tell me…
PRESENT	Yes?
BOB	Fee, Fie, Ho, Hum, I smell the scent of an empty tum!

Martha's giggles give the game away and her father finds her and tickles her.

MARTHA	Stop it!

Mrs Cratchit places the goose on the table to great applause.

BOB   Daughter, sit and eat the feast that Mr Scrooge has provided!

Scrooge raises an eyebrow at the spirit in arrogance and smirks. The Spirit casts a withering look at him and then at the gathered Cratchit family.

Pause.

They are silent and sullen.

BOB   We should not be ungrateful.

MRS CRATCHIT   No. He is the ingrate!

BOB   A merry Christmas to us all. God bless us!

TINY TIM   Happy Christmas! God bless us every one!

Scrooge wipes a tear from his eye.

The spirit looks at him with disparagement.

SCROOGE   What a lovely child. *Beat.* Spirit. Tell me, will Tiny Tim live?

PRESENT   I see a vacant seat in the poor chimney corner, and a crutch without an owner, carefully preserved. If these shadows remain unaltered by the Future, the child will die.

SCROOGE   No. No. Oh No! Kind Spirit! Say he will be spared.

PRESENT   If these shadows remain unaltered by the Future none other of my race will find him here. What then? *Beat.* If he be destined to die, he had better do it, and 'decrease the surplus population'.

The spirit fixes Scrooge with a look of withering contempt and scorn.

SCROOGE   Surplus?

PRESENT   Your words man. *Beat.* Will you decide what men shall live, and what men shall die? *Beat.* It may be that, in the sight of Heaven, you are more worthless and less fit to live than this poor man's child. *Beat.* Oh God! To hear the insect on the leaf pronouncing on the too much life among his hungry brothers in the dust!

BOB   Mr Scrooge! The founder of the feast!

They all sit reticent and skulking.

MRS CRATCHIT   You mention his name in this house as a provider!

BOB   My dear, *beat,* Merry Christmas!

They raise their glasses and toast.

ALL: Merry Christmas!

They all toast to be at one with their father and provider.

Scrooge watches them tuck in with a glum glee. He looks at the spirit who is engrossed in their temporary happiness.

SCROOGE   A fine family!

PRESENT   Indeed.

The spirit sullenly cast his and about with more sprinkling dust, the world goes dark and is surrounded by the sound of crashing waves.

Scene 5

A ship at sea, sound of waves hurtling about the tiny fisher boat.

Phantoms are singing and the sirens wailing the hymn: 'For those who die upon the sea…'

A young sailor stands watch, buffeted by the wind.

The spirit sprinkles his magic…

The Captain, a wizened old man, appears on the deck with a lantern and two mugs of grog.

He hands one to the young sailor and clinks his own against it.

CAPTAIN	Merry Christmas!
SAILOR	Merry Christmas captain!

They look out to sea together and sup, and grin.

PRESENT	It doesn't take much…
SCROOGE	Do they make it to shore?
PRESENT	As if you care?

Scrooge bows his head in shame.

PRESENT	Lest their widows are a drain on your taxes and generosity?
SCROOGE	Enough!
PRESENT	Even Poseidon would be loath to drown a man on this day…
SCROOGE	No, of course.

PRESENT	Unless he wanted a day off…
SCROOGE	Spirit!
PRESENT	Whether they live or die is beyond your jurisdiction…
SCROOGE	Take me home please, I'm weary. I'll pay any…
PRESENT	One more shadow. You know you want to…
SCROOGE	No!

The spirit sprinkles his dust and all is changed.

Scene 6.

Fred and his beloved wife, Betty, plus guests of Topper and Helen have just finished dinner and are in party mood.

FRED	He said that Christmas was a humbug. *Beat.* He believed it too!
BETTY	Shame on him Fred.
SCROOGE	Women! *Beat.* Bless them. They never do anything by halves, they are always in earnest.
PRESENT	So…*(Chuckling)* You understand women?
SCROOGE	I just said…
TOPPER	I hear he is very rich.
BETTY	His wealth is of no use to him.
FRED	He's a comical old fellow. I feel sorry for him.

BETTY	Soppy fool!
FRED	I couldn't be angry with him if I tried. Who is it that suffers by his mood? *Beat.* Himself always. He takes it into his head to dislike us, and he won't come and dine with us. What's the consequence? *Beat.* A wonderful dinner amongst kith and kin, that's what.
HELEN	It is his loss indeed. Your only relative too…
FRED	I intend to give him the opportunity every year, whether he likes it or not! *Beat.* A toast!

They all raise their glasses.

FRED	Uncle Scrooge!

They all look at him, he is insistent.

ALL	Uncle Scrooge!
TOPPER	A game?

They all applaud and sit ready and expectant.

HELEN	The 'yes and no' game!

Scrooge rubs his hands with glee. Fred is first to stand up and act out the role.

SCROOGE	I love party games!
PRESENT	No you don't! Time grows ever short.
SCROOGE	This is a new game. A little time…please?

Rapid fire questioning now from the party, to which Fred may only answer 'yes' or 'no' until they guess who he is.

TOPPER	Female?
FRED	No.
HELEN	Happy?
FRED	No.
BETTY	Dead?
FRED	*Beat.* No.
SCROOGE	I wonder who it could be?

The spirit raises his eyebrows at the engrossed Scrooge, and raises his arms to sprinkle his magic. Darkness falls..

Scene 7

A choir of paupers sing 'Silent Night', dolefully by the town Christmas Tree. Rosie, covered in frost, shivers, and takes her final match and strikes it for warmth and temporary escape. She starts to smile as she dreams.

The spirit lets out a sigh. Scrooge looks at him quizzically.

SCROOGE	Are spirits' lives so short?
PRESENT	My life upon this globe is very brief. It ends tonight.
SCROOGE	The girl who sells matches at my door…She has expands her business. *Beat.* She will thrive?

The spirit points the doorstep and lights up the doorway where Rosie is frozen stiff with smile on her lifeless face.

PRESENT   My time ends tonight at midnight. *Beat.* Hark! The time is drawing near.

During the twelve chimes, two children, Want, a boy, and Ignorance, a girl, appear and attach themselves to the spirit's cloak. The lights dim as the bells ring out.

SCROOGE   Who are these wretches?

PRESENT   Look upon them.

SCROOGE   Are they yours?

PRESENT   They are Man's. *Beat.* This boy is ignorance and the girl is want. *Beat.* Beware them both, but especially the boy; for I see on his brow all that is written which is doom – unless the writing be erased. Deny it! *Beat.* Admit your factious purposes and make it worse! Then bide the ending!

The spirit raises his arms towards Heaven.

SCROOGE   Have they a refuge or not?

The spirit places his arms about the children's shoulders.

PRESENT   Are there no prisons? Are there no workhouses?

The final bell rings out. The spirit is no more. Darkness.

Act IV

Scene 1

Scrooge in his rocking chair. The clock hands spin wildly.

A phantom dressed in a black robe with hood appears silently in the room and the clock freezes. The spirit holds out a hand towards Scrooge.

Scrooge senses the presence, grimaces, and turns to look up at the spirit.

SCROOGE   I am in the presence of Christmas yet to come?

The spirit remains silent but gestures onward with its hand.

SCROOGE   You are about to show me shadows of the things that have not happened, but will happen in the future. *Beat.* Is that so spirit?

The spirit inclines its head slowly by way of answer.

SCROOGE   Oh ghost of the future, I fear you more than any spectre I have seen. But, as I know your purpose is to do me good, and as I hope to live to be another man from what I was, I am prepared to be in your company, and do so with a grateful heart. Will you not speak to me?

The spirit lets out a deep moan and waves its hand, gesturing onwards.

SCROOGE   Lead on! *Beat.* Lead on!

Darkness.

Scene 2

Scrooge and the spirit are now in the town square. He looks at his doorway, it is empty.

Two businessmen wander on.

BUSINESSMAN # 1 I only know he's dead, that's all.

BUSINESSMAN # 2 When did he die?

BUSINESSMAN # 1 Last night I believe…

BUSINESSMAN # 2 On Christmas Eve!

BUSINESSMAN # 1 Well he never did like Christmas.

BUSINESSMAN # 2 What was the matter with him?

BUSINESSMAN # 1 *(Yawning)* God knows!

BUSINESSMAN # 2 What has he done with all his money?

BUSINESSMAN # 1 He hasn't left it to me, I know that much.

The men guffaw.

BUSINESSMAN # 2 The funeral is likely to be a cheap affair. I don't envisage a crowd. Perhaps we should go along for fun?

BUSINESSMAN # 1 And a free supper!

BUSINESSMAN # 2 Why not? That'll make the covetous old sinner spin in his grave!

BUSINESSMAN # 1 I suppose I should, I was a friend, well, an acquaintance. We used to stop and speak whenever we met.

BUSINESSMAN # 2   His only friend in the world then! Let's go. *Beat.* I'll wager that we're the only ones there bar the gravediggers and the priest.

Scrooge shakes his head.

SCROOGE   Poor wretch! To be mocked and mourned so…

The phantom inclines his head and waves an arm imperiously, shrouding all in darkness.

Scene 3

A den of iniquity and squalor.

Old Joe holds court as the three thieves enter one by one to show him their plunder. They cackle in a conspiratorial fashion. Mrs Dilber holds a bundle of cloth, Mrs Widdle, with a blanket full of trinkets, Mr Smith, the undertaker's man, in faded black and top hat, clasps a knotted handkerchief.

OLD JOE   Welcome to my parlour!

Scrooge recoils from the stench and places a handkerchief about his face to stifle it.

MRS WIDDLE   What odds on this Mrs Dilber? You too Mr Smith!

MRS DILBER   Every person has a right to take care of themselves, Mrs Widdle. *Beat.* He always did!

MRS WIDDLE   No man more so!

MR SMITH   Don't be afraid gentle women. No one's the wiser. I should know, but two strangers at his burial.

OLD JOE	Let Mrs Dilber the noble laundress go first, then Mrs Widdle, the charwoman, and we'll end on high with Mr Smith, the undertaker's man, an undertaking that is brisk nowadays…
MRS WIDDLE	Very well, who's the worse for the loss of a few things like these? Not a dead man, I suppose?
MRS DILBER	Indeed!
MRS WIDDLE	If he wanted to keep 'em after he was gone, wicked old screw, then why wasn't he natural in his lifetime?

They all nod their agreement, none more so than Old Joe who eyes their wares expectantly.

MRS DILBER	If he had been, he'd have somebody to look after him when Death struck – instead of lying their, alone, gasping out his last, all alone by himself.
MRS WIDDLE	Truest word ever spoke. *Beat.* It is a judgement upon him.
MRS DILBER	I wish it was a heavier judgement, and it should have been. *Beat.* I am not afraid to be the first…Open it, open the bundle Old Joe.

There is no gallantry in this 'parlour' however, and Mr Smith jangles his 'offering' and unties his handkerchief. Gold teeth and cufflinks spill out onto the table.

MR SMITH	Time is of the essence as they say…

The spirit turns to Scrooge and nods his tacit agreement.

MR SMITH   Where he's headed he won't be needing these! *Beat.* They'd only melt in the fire...His very own gnashers!

The two women recoil in horror.

MRS DILBER   Mr Smith! You didn't! Not his own false fangs.

Mr Smith gives a toothy grin and holds up a pair of pliers, he plays with them and makes for their teeth too. They all cackle and Old Joe gathers them up quickly, then bites on one to test its validity. Old Joe nods his approval. He makes a note on a scrap of paper.

OLD JOE   This will be a profitable night for all of us I feel. Who said the spirit of Christmas was dead?

A sick cackle from the assembled, the two women keen to show their wares. They scuffle to show Old Joe their spoils. Mrs Widdle elbows Mrs Dilber out of the way.

OLD JOE   Next!

MRS WIDDLE   Here you go Joe! Feast your eyes on this little lot!

A pocket watch, and trinkets fall onto the table. Old Joe snaps the watch up and listens.

OLD JOE   Umm...Still ticking! *Beat.* Unlike his cold old ticker!

Old Joe scribbles on his pad and grins. The others chuckle manically.

MR SMITH   He'll be marking time where he's going and that's a fact...

OLD JOE   You ladies, a soft spot, that's what I have. I'll pay you well for this little bit of booty.

Mrs Widdle coos her appreciation and pecks Old Joe on the cheek.

Scrooge checks his own waistcoat, the pocket watch is still there. He sighs gratefully.

MRS DILBER   Now look at my bundle, please Joe.

Old Joe unravels her bundle and holds up a fine silk shirt to the light, then recoils.

OLD JOE   Hope he didn't die of anything catching?

MRS DILBER   No holes in that shirt. They'd have wasted it if it hadn't been for me.

OLD JOE   What do you call wasting of it?

MRS DILBER   Putting it on him to be buried in, to be sure. *Beat.* Somebody was fool enough to do it, but I took it off again. If calico ain't good enough for such a purpose, it isn't good enough for anything. It's even quite becoming to the body. He can't look uglier than he did in that one.

SCROOGE   I do not want to go the way of this poor unfortunate. Take me home, I beg you…

OLD JOE   Ha ha! This is the end of it. He frightened everyone away from him when he was alive, to profit us, dear friends, when was dead. Ha!

The spirit waves a hand at Old Joe – he becomes entranced, and stands like an automaton.

SCROOGE (O/S)   I beg you spirit!

OLD JOE			Tick Tock!

The old conspirators gather together and stand in formation. The spirit starts to clap his hands, and they start to march on the spot, in time to his beat.

The spirit clicks its fingers: The four conspirators freeze.

The 'phantom choir' march on and surround the four 'friends'. The bell starts to toll. Scrooge covers his ears.

ALL			Tick! Tock! The old screw is dead,
			No one mourns him, not even Fred.
			He got what he deserves, a place in hell;
			He marks times alone, to the toll of the bell.

			Tick! Tock! He is dead, there'll be others,
			The Devil will be fed…
			Not the poor, weak or young:
			They are trifles, manure and dung.

			Tick! Tock! Chance, chance, chance to mend,
			Choose money, my dear, my very dear friend.
			But there is a price, a cost to this:
			The wandering of the world, alone, abysss…

All start to hiss and mark time. The spirit waves his arm, clicks his fingers, and they march off at his command.

Scrooge tugs at the spirits' cloak with one free hand.

SCROOGE		I see! I see! The case of this unhappy man might be my own. My life tends that way now…

The Spirit waves its arms and casts all into shadow.

Scene 4

A gloomy room, a dead man, covered by a threadbare sheet. An icy foot protrudes. An eerie lights up the body. Scrooge recoils in terror.

The spirit groans a lament.

Scrooge looks pleadingly at the spirit.

SCROOGE   Merciful Heaven! *Beat.* What is this?

The spirit merely points at the corpse's head.

SCROOGE   This is a fearful place Spirit! In leaving it, I shall not leave its lesson. Trust me! Let us go!

Scrooge is reluctant to investigate, he looks at his guide.

SCROOGE   I understand you and I would do it if I could. But I don't have the power, spirit. I just don't have the power.

The spirit merely points at it again. Scrooge makes to touch the shroud but can't.

SCROOGE   This is too much...

The spirit inclines his head at the body. Scrooge closes his eyes and clasps the sheet. He just can't bear to look and falls to his knees, his hands clasped together towards the spirit.

SCROOGE   If there is anyone in this town who feels more emotion at this man's death, then show them to me. Oh spirit! I beseech you!

The spirit casts his arms up in despair, groans, and all is in darkness once more.

Scene 5

A young impoverished woman, Caroline, sits nursing her infant in a rocking chair.

She glances at the clock nervously. Her husband, Jim, enters with a flourish.

JIM   I have news!

CAROLINE   Is it good or bad?

JIM   Bad!

CAROLINE   We are quite ruined?

JIM   No! There is hope yet, my dear Caroline…

CAROLINE   A miracle! Nothing is past help, he has relented?

JIM   I don't know about that! He is well past that! *Beat.* He is dead!

Caroline kisses her babe's head and cheers. Jim holds his hands high. She relents and starts to pray.

CAROLINE   I'm sorry, I shouldn't…

JIM   A drunken old laundress told me the news, quite ecstatic she was, and quite drunk. *Beat.* Binge drinking gin no doubt. *Beat.* Anyway, what we thought was an excuse to avoid my excuses was quite true. He was not only ill, but dying!

Jim punches a fist into the air.

CAROLINE   To whom will the debt be transferred?

JIM   I have no idea, but whoever inherits our debt, it will at least be past Christmas before they come for it. *Beat.* Whatever happens to it, it can't pass to colder hands…

Scrooge is beside himself with angst and tugs at the spirit's robes.

SCROOGE   Let me see some tenderness with a death, or that dark chamber which we left just now, will be ever in my mind.

The spirit waves its arms and casts its shadow.

Scene 6

Bob Cratchit's house – now solemn and dim.

The Cratchits sits at their table but there is an empty seat. A lonely crutch stands by its side. Mrs Cratchit and Belinda sow stoically. Martha stirs the broth. Peter stands at his father's side reading, Bob, who stares into the abyss of the empty space.

PETER   And he took a child and set him in the midst of them…

The phantom choir start to lurk in every nook and cranny of the Cratchit kitchen.

Bob Cratchit starts to sob quietly to himself.

SCROOGE   Where is the little boy?

The spirit growls at him.

SCROOGE   Tiny Tim?

The spirit lifts the crutch and the Cratchit family freeze.

The spirit conducts the phantom choir with the crutch.

PHANTOMS   Gone, gone, to a place on high.
           Beware the phantom: Fie! Fie! Fie!

           Love is not enough, to fill our tum.
           For us there is no happy drum.

           Death stalks all, even the good…
           Beware his glare, bright, from his hood.

           He is at your shoulder, watching your move
           Your last chance of past actions to disprove…

The spirit throws the crutch at Scrooge and waits. Scrooge examines it guiltily then replaces it. The Cratchits are reanimated.

Mrs Cratchit lays her sewing on the table and places a consoling arm around her husband.

MRS CRATCHIT   Don't grieve so.

BOB   My shoulders feel light, yet my heart heavy.

MRS CRATCHIT   We shall visit him again tonight.

BOB   Our little child!

ALL   Our little child!

The family embrace and seem to look at Scrooge who shuffles uncomfortably. Scrooge tugs at the spirit's robes.

SCROOGE   We can go now, surely?

The spirit shrugs him off.

BOB   I met Master Fred this afternoon. The kindest of gentleman, who commiserated with our loss and gave me his card. He also asked after my good wife. *Beat.* How did he know that?

MRS CRATCHIT   What dear?

BOB   Why, that I had a good wife…

MRS CRATCHIT   Everybody knows that!

The family starts to chuckle, even Bob smiles at his dear wife.

BOB   Whatever happens, however and whenever we part from one another, I am sure we shall, none of us, forget poor Tiny Tim.

ALL   Never, father!

BOB   When we recollect how patient and mild he was, although he was a little, little child; we shall not quarrel easily amongst ourselves, and forget poor Tiny Tim in doing it.

ALL   No. *Beat.* Never father!

BOB   I am very happy!

They all embrace again and freeze in a picture of family warmth.

SCROOGE   Spectre! Something tells me that our parting moment is at hand. I know it but I know not how. Tell me what man that was whom we saw lying dead?

The spirit lifts his cloak and all is shrouded in gloom.

Scene 7

A churchyard, the untended tombstones are overgrown and covered in weeds. The phantoms lurk in shadows.

The spirit stands among the graves and points to one in particular.

SCROOGE   Before I draw near to that stone to which you point. Answer me one question. Are these the shadows of the things that will be, or are they shadows of the things that may be only?

The spirit points once more at the grave, a light waves briefly over it.

SCROOGE   Men's courses will foreshadow certain ends, to which, if persevered in, must lead. But if the courses be departed from, the ends will change. Say it is thus with what you show me!

The spirit is as immovable as ever.

Scrooge creeps trembling towards it. The light from the spirit reveals the name: Ebenezer Scrooge.

Scrooge falls to his knees and sobs.

SCROOGE   Am I that man who lay upon the bed?

The spirit points from the grave to Scrooge and back again.

SCROOGE   No! Spirit no!

The spirit stands pointing at the headstone.

SCROOGE   Hear me. I am not the man I was. Why show me this, if I am past all hope?

The spirit holds his hands up in the air.

SCROOGE   Your nature intercedes for me, and pities me. Assure me that I yet may change these shadows you have shown me by an altered life?

The spirit beckons to the phantoms. They stand and move to the fore.

The spirit clicks his fingers and the phantoms part.

Rosie appears as a ghost, deathly white, and passes through them.

Scrooge points to her in recognition.

SCROOGE   I know her, the little match girl…

The spirit holds a finger to his lips. Rosie starts to conduct the phantom choir.

PHANTOMS   How indeed to avoid the wrath?
                    Stumble upon a better path.

                    Leaves a match girl to die alone in cold.
                    How he asks questions – so inanely bold.

                    Aphrodite herself could not change,
                    A heart that only in wealth did range.

                    This heart so cold, and now contrite
                    Who is to know what wrong, what right?

                    Will he live or will he die?
                    Hell gives out a welcoming sigh!

Rosie then nods to the spirit and withdraws through the phantoms.

Scrooge calls out after her.

SCROOGE   Wait girl!

The phantoms advance and start to move ethereally about Scrooge.

SCROOGE   I will honour Christmas in my heart, and try to keep it all year. *Beat.* I will live in the Past, the Present and the Future! The spirits of all three shall strive within me. I will not shut out the lessons they teach. Oh, tell me I may sponge away the writing on this stone.

Scrooge tries to take the spirit's hand. The spirit withdraws.

The spirit holds up its arms to heaven. Scrooge freezes. The phantoms carry him off.

Darkness.

Act V

Scene 1

Scrooge's office. He is in his rocking chair. The office is as normal bar one change: Marley's portrait is now grinning.

Scrooge is now a changed man: cheerful and light of soul and foot.

He stands up, peers about him and pinches himself.

SCROOGE   I will live in the Past, the Present and the Future!

He dances a jig.

SCROOGE   The spirits of all three shall strive within me.

He addresses the portrait.

SCROOGE   Oh, Jacob Marley! Heaven and the Christmastime be praised for this! I say it on my knees, old Jacob; on my knees!

He gets up and walks in circles.

SCROOGE   I am here. *Beat.* The shadows of the things that would have been may be dispelled. They will be. I know they will!

The church bells toll.

SCROOGE   It's all right! It all true, it all happened, but I am still here! *Pause.* But what day is it? How long have I been among the spirits? I don't know anything.

He approaches the door and tentatively opens it. Rosie slowly looks up at him, her face covered in frost.

SCROOGE   You're alive. Dear child, what day is it?

ROSIE	Today! Why it's Christmas day!
SCROOGE	Christmas day! I haven't missed it! The spirits have done it all in one night. They can do anything they like. Of course the can. *Beat.* Come in dear child!

Rosie is reluctant and watches him warily.

ROSIE	Mr Scrooge?
SCROOGE	Scrooge but not Scrooge. Ha Ha!

He empties his safe of coins and grabs his coat. He gives her his coat.

SCROOGE	Do you know the poulterer's around the corner?
ROSIE	I do.
SCROOGE	Clever girl. Do you know whether they've sold the prize turkey that was hanging up there?
ROSIE	The one that is even bigger than me. I have gazed at it only last night.
SCROOGE	What a delightful child. It's a pleasure talking to you. Now, go and buy it!

Rosie looks at him as if he is bonkers.

ROSIE	Help!
SCROOGE	No! No! I'm in earnest. Bring it back in five minutes and you shall have a half a crown.

Rosie is unsure what to do. Scrooge hands her some coins and takes her last box of matches.

ROSIE	But the box is now empty. I used them to keep warm last night.

SCROOGE	Honest too! You shall be Bob's assistant! *Beat.* Now go!

Rosie shoots off. Scrooge laughs manically to himself.

SCROOGE	I'll send it to Bob Cratchit's. He shan't know who sends it. It's twice the size of Tiny Tim.

Scrooge continues chuckling to himself. Christabel and Holly peer in the open door and look at each other.

Scrooge notices them and beckons them in.

SCROOGE	Come in! Come in! Merry Christmas Ladies!

HOLLY	Mr Scrooge?

Scrooge notices a sprig of mistletoe on Holly's lapel. He snatches it and holds it up.

SCROOGE	I've changed! Call me Ebenezer! *Beat.* Give me a Christmas kiss. *Beat.* You beauties!

The two sisters withdraw nervously.

CHRISTABEL	That's what they all say when they want a kiss and a cuddle!

SCROOGE	No, I really have…

Scrooge holds the mistletoe aloft, closes his eyes and puckers up for kiss.

HOLLY   I don't know, he seems to have a twinkle in his eye!

CHRISTABEL   He's been at the grog! This Ebenezer has become quite a sleazer!

Holly gives him a tentative peck on the cheek. He is ecstatic and starts a merry dance, holding his heart.

SCROOGE   Come to my nephew's. There is a party! They have games too!

HOLLY   Spin the bottle no doubt. *Beat.* Let us go sister.

Rosie appears behind an enormous turkey. Scrooge hands her a coin.

SCROOGE   Good girl. *Beat.* Take it to Bob Cratchit's. You know where he lives?

ROSIE   I do.

Rosie struggles with the enormous turkey. He hands her another coin and holds the door for her.

SCROOGE   Why you can't carry that all the way to Camden Town. Take a cab!

Rosie sets off. The two sisters regard each other and raise their eyebrows.

SCROOGE   Now ladies, we must discuss your charity. It's such important work you do. Count me in!

CHRISTABEL   We will!

HOLLY   Bless you Mr Scrooge!

SCROOGE	Back payments too. It must be a full and fair account.

Scrooge looks at the portrait of Marley and sniggers. He takes a dusty bottle from behind the cabinet and blows on to it. A great deal of dust, then darkness…

Scene 2

Fred's house. Fred, Betty, Topper and Helen are at dinner. There is a knock at the door.

Fred is astonished to see his uncle.

SCROOGE	Fred!
FRED	Uncle!

Scrooge hands his nephew the bottle.

SCROOGE	It's I. Your uncle Scrooge. I have come to dinner. Will you let me in, Fred?

Fred grabs his uncle by the hand, they shake and embrace. He shows his uncle proudly to the astonished guests.

SCROOGE	Happy Christmas!
ALL	*(Somewhat flummoxed)* Happy Christmas!
FRED	Take a seat.
SCROOGE	I hope you don't mind dear Fred, but I have taken the liberty of inviting a couple of lady friends to join us later.
BETTY	Friends?
TOPPER	Lady friends?

Fred grins at his wife and pats his uncle on the shoulder.

FRED	I am glad for you uncle, truly I am.

Scene 3

Scrooge's office, Boxing Day.

Rosie is at Bob's desk scribing away. Scrooge is dictating a letter.

SCROOGE	The monthly payment will hereby be reduced to an amount to your suiting. *Beat.* Yours etc.

Rosie adds the letter to the pile.

SCROOGE	How many more?

Rosie scours the ledger.

ROSIE	A good few, Mr Scrooge.

The clock strikes half nine.

Bob enters in a hurry, unwrapping himself from hat and scarf. He eyes his desk nervously.

BOB	Hallo...So sorry Mr Scrooge. I...

SCROOGE	Hallo! What do you mean by coming here at this time of day?

BOB	I am very sorry, sir. I am behind...

SCROOGE	You are. Step this way, sir.

BOB	It's only once a year, sir. It shall not happen again. I was making rather merry, sir.

SCROOGE   Now I'll tell you something, my friend. I am not going to stand for this sort of thing any longer, and so…

Bob is trembling. Scrooge digs him in the ribs playfully.

SCROOGE   And so…you've been replaced!

BOB   Sir?

SCROOGE   You've been promoted!

BOB   Sir?

SCROOGE   I am therefore going to raise your salary!

Bob still trembles, unsure. Rosie looks at him with a warm smile.

ROSIE   It's true.

SCROOGE   A merry Christmas, Bob!

BOB   Merry Christmas, Mr Scrooge!

SCROOGE   A merrier Christmas, Bob, than I have given you for many year. *Beat.* I'll raise your salary, and endeavour to assist your struggling family. We will discuss your affairs this very afternoon, over a bowl of mulled wine.

BOB   Sir!

The phantoms appear by the side of the stage watching Scrooge.

Scrooge shivers and bows his thanks with a wide grin. He is truly a changed man.

SCROOGE   Now run along and buy some coal, stoke up the fires!

The phantoms start to sway merrily and hum.

Mrs Cratchit and Tiny Tim arrive nervously with a packed lunch for Bob.

Bob whispers his news to his wife and son. They look at Scrooge appreciatively.

MRS CRATCHIT   God bless you, Mr Scrooge!

Scrooge bows politely.

SCROOGE   Bless you and yours, Mrs Cratchit!

TINY TIM   God bless us every one!

Tiny Tim holds his crutch aloft. The cast freeze.

The phantoms swarm onto the stage and sprinkle glitter over a picture of happiness in Scrooge's office.

Happy Christmas, everyone!

The End

All rights reserved. © Copyright Ed Scates 2008

Printed in Poland
by Amazon Fulfillment
Poland Sp. z o.o., Wrocław